Sweet Dreams to you!
Rose Lewis

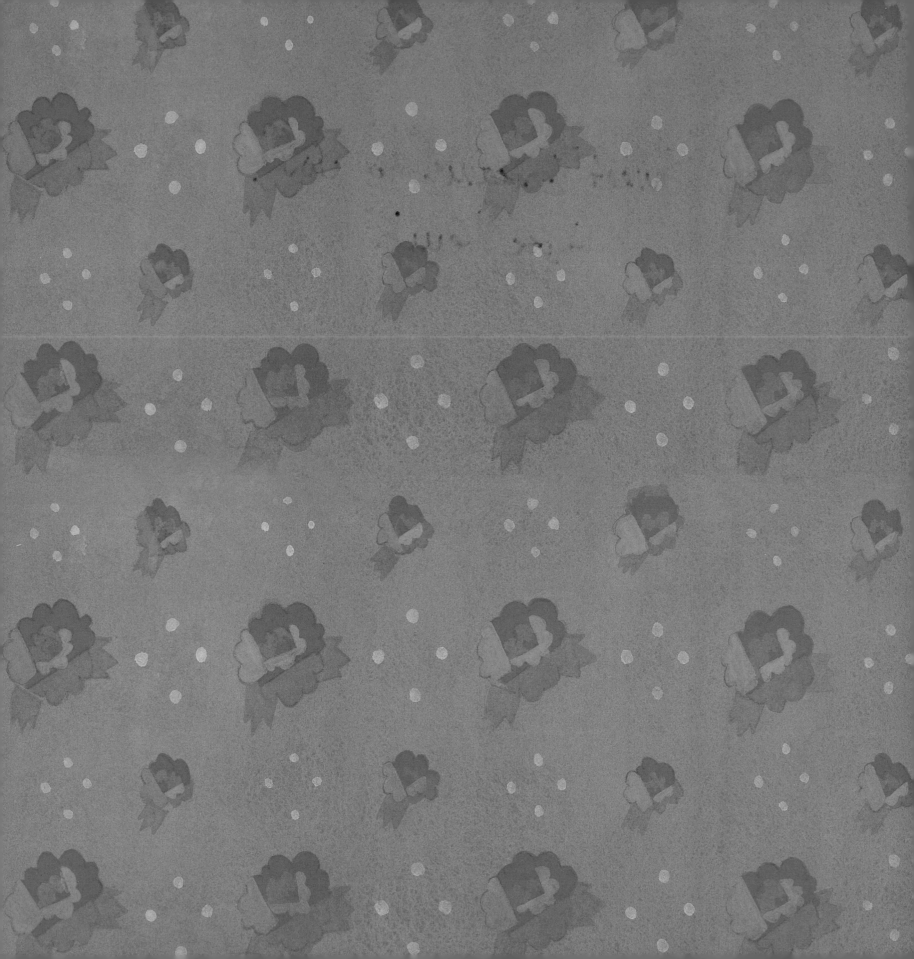

SWEET DREAMS

By

Rose A. Lewis

Illustrated by

Jen Corace

ABRAMS BOOKS FOR YOUNG READERS, NEW YORK

Good night, my precious child,

May your dreams be long and sweet—

And full of great adventures

With the friends you're soon to meet.

Up in the sky is Mr. Moon,

Who'll watch you through the night—

His very round and smiling face

Shines beautiful and bright.

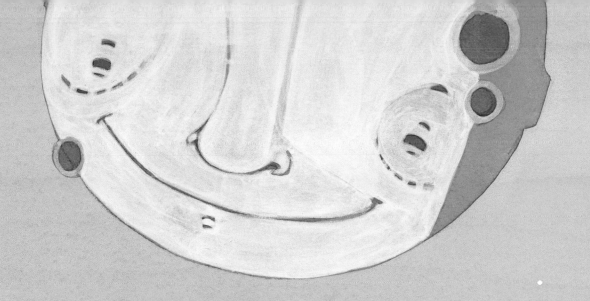

Nighttime says a quick "Sleep tight"

To the fading morning glories—

Then wakes up all the moonflowers

And listens to their stories.

Like the one about the baby bear

Simply much too tired to eat,

Who made the moonflowers' petals

A pillow for his feet.

And the very teeny, tiny mouse

Soaking wet from a big puddle,

Curled up under the moonflowers' vines,

Just waiting for a cuddle.

Then there are the baby birds

Comforting each other.

They're sitting in their nest alone

And waiting for their mother.

She's gone to fetch some dinner

But will return home very soon—

Flying through the nighttime sky

With the help of Mr. Moon.

The butterflies have gone to sleep,

Their wings no longer flapping,

Making room for the nighttime moths,

Their soft gray wings now tapping.

And from the field a symphony—

The crickets sing their song.

Their nighttime friends their audience,

From moonrise until dawn.

You see, my precious child,

Not all friends sleep at night.

Some come alive in darkness—

They have no need of light.

But when the nighttime passes,

And Mr. Moon nods off to sleep,

Say good morning to Miss Sunshine

And the company she keeps.

There are daisies that are dancing

To the sounds of singing robins,

And the ducks all gathered on the pond

With their little heads a-bobbin'.

There are beautiful red roses

Shaking off the morning dew.

You see, they're all quite busy

Making a new day just for you.

So let me say good night again

With a kiss upon your head—

As you're drifting off to dreamland,

Warm and snuggled in your bed.

Good night, my precious child,

May your dreams be long and sweet—

And full of great adventures

With the friends you're soon to meet.